Pokémon

HOW TO DRAW

ADVENTURES

HOW TO DRAW
ADVENTURES

Written by Maria S. Barbo   Illustrated by Ron Zalme

SCHOLASTIC INC.

CONTENTS

INTRODUCTION

Ready to start your drawing journey?
PACK YOUR DRAWING KIT!

What you'll need:

- Pencils
- Paper
- Erasers
- A thin black marker

You may also want:

- Scrap paper
- A sketchbook (with your name on it!)
- A straightedge or ruler
- Something with a round base, like a cup
- Colored pencils, crayons, markers, or watercolors
- Snacks!

Each drawing starts general—with the simplest shapes—and gets more detailed as you go.

WARM UP!

Wanna know a secret? Every drawing of a Pokémon starts off the same way—even the ones that seem really hard! They all begin with simple lines and basic shapes. So, train before you strain!

Challenge #1: How many different kinds of lines can you draw in one minute? Pull out a piece of scrap paper, set a timer, and draw lines for one minute. See any squiggles, zigzags, sweeping curves, or straight, wiggly, wavy, or jagged lines? What might an anxious line look like? What about a powerful line?

Challenge #2: How many different kinds of shapes can you draw? Squint your eyes and take a look at this drawing of Scorbunny. Does squinting help you break the drawing down into its basic shapes? Practice drawing circles, squares, rectangles, triangles, and hexagons on scrap paper. Ready, set, go!

Start with light, loose lines in case you have to erase them. Finish off with darker, heavier lines once you've decided which lines will stay and which will go!

BACK TO BASICS

In this book, you'll start every Pokémon by drawing two crisscrossing guidelines. Sometimes they'll be curved to show motion and dimension. Sometimes they'll be straight. But they'll always be there.

GUIDELINES

Guidelines help you figure out where to draw different details and shapes. This vertical guideline runs down the middle of Scorbunny's body like a spine. This horizontal guideline shows you where to place the basic shapes of the nose, eyes, ears, belly, arms, and feet.

HOW TO DRAW FACES

Guidelines also help you draw faces. Check this out.

1. Start with two guidelines.

2. Draw a circle for the head. See how the guidelines break the circle up into sections? Scorbunny will not be looking straight at you, so the guidelines are not in the middle of the circle.

3. See how the eyes sit on the horizontal guideline? Place one eye on each side of the vertical guideline.

4. Draw the nose where the guidelines cross.

5. The mouth is on the bottom section of the face.

6. Now that you've sketched all the basic shapes, start adding details. There is an oval inside each eye. And two curved lines inside the mouth for the teeth and tongue.

7. Ta-da! Erase the guidelines and you are done!

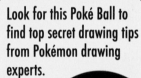
Look for this Poké Ball to find top secret drawing tips from Pokémon drawing experts.

TIME OUT!
Remember, you can always pause to practice shapes and complicated details on scrap paper!

Let's get started!

MANTYKE

This friendly Pokémon looks like a mini version of its evolved form, Mantine. Mantyke is good at special attack moves. It's also a great Pokémon to try drawing first. Mantyke's body looks like a big circle with fins. Can you tell why it's known as the Kite Pokémon?

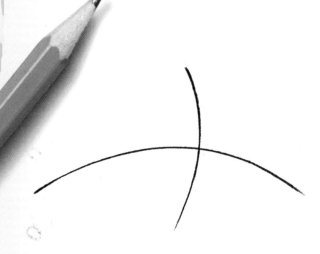

1 Start by drawing two guidelines that crisscross and curve. Keep them really light so you can erase them later on.

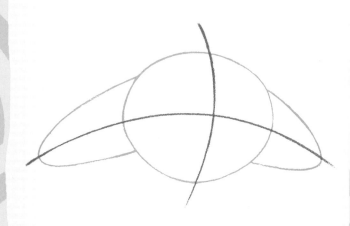

2 Draw a big oval on top of the lines. The two lines meet in the middle of the oval. Then use the horizontal guideline to help you position the fins.

3 Use the lines from step one as a guide to place the eyes and mouth. Then draw two antenna feelers at the top of Mantyke's oval body.

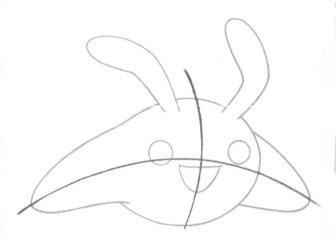

4 It's time to add details! Draw the curving line that runs around Mantyke's body. Then add another line for the tongue. Finally, darken the details on Mantyke's bright happy eyes.

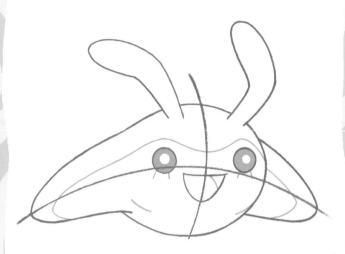

5 You did it! Your first Pokémon drawing is almost done. Erase the guidelines from step one and any other lines you don't need. Now take a minute to fine-tune the outline of the body.

6 Chase away the blues . . . with color! Color in Mantyke with two different shades of blue. Then go back and trace over the lines with a thin black marker.

GREAT JOB!
You've just powered through your first Pokémon drawing challenge. Keep up the good work!

PIKACHU

Ash's Pikachu has been his constant companion ever since the Trainer started his Pokémon journey. Pikachu is awfully cute, but as everyone knows, you don't want to mess with its Electric-type attacks!

1 From top to bottom, Pikachu's head is about the same size as its body. Remember that, and you'll have a top-notch Pikachu.

2 Where would Pikachu be without its lightning-bolt-shaped tail? Use straight lines to draw the tail peeking out from behind its body. Give Pikachu five tiny fingers on each hand and three toes on each foot. The lines on Pikachu's ears show where the yellow stops and the black tips begin.

3

Erase the extra outlines. Add two circles for Pikachu's cheeks. Make sure the circles are attached to the sides of the face.

4

Give Pikachu a smiling mouth. Then add two circles for eyes. Make sure they are smaller than the circles for Pikachu's cheeks, and try not to draw them too close together.

5

Draw two smaller circles inside the eyes for pupils. Leave these white, and color in the rest in black. Draw a small mark for a nose and fill in the black tips of Pikachu's ears. Finally, add detail to Pikachu's tail. *Aww.* Don't you just want to give it a hug?

DRAWING TIP:

Now that you've gotten the hang of drawing Pikachu, why not try drawing it in other poses?

PIKACHU IN ACTION

Pikachu is always on the move—especially when there are whole new regions to explore! Now that you've practiced Pikachu, try drawing the Electric-type Pokémon leaping into action! Is your Pikachu about to start a battle or jump into a pile of berries? You decide!

1 Lightly sketch two crisscrossing guidelines for the body. Then draw a circle for the head. Most of the circle should sit above the horizontal guideline. When you're ready, draw a curved line on the face where the eyes will be.

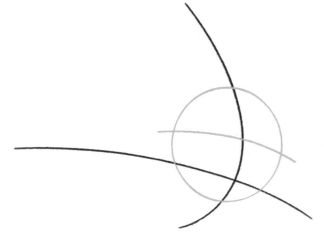

2 Use this step to block in the simplest shapes. Pikachu's body looks a little like a jellybean. Draw it around the horizontal guideline. Then draw two circles for eyes and a wavy line for the top of the mouth. Did you notice that Pikachu's ears are blowing back in the wind?

3

Draw a starter shape for the tail behind Pikachu's right ear. Then lightly sketch the right hand and foot. Add details like the bottom curve of the mouth, the circles in the eyes, and the stripes on Pikachu's back. Don't forget the curved line inside its mouth for the tongue!

4

Connect the tail shape to the body with zigzagging lines. Can you spot the zigzags in Pikachu's paws as well? Don't forget circles on its cheeks. Pikachu can't use Thundershock without them!

DRAWING TIP
The guidelines in this drawing curve to the right because Pikachu is moving in that direction.

5

Time for finishing touches like color and background! But first, erase the lines you don't need and make any changes you want. Did you catch the detail at the tip of the ears? If you use markers for color, prevent bleeding by letting the yellow dry before adding darker colors.

DRAWING TIP:

Practice your Pikachu by tracing the final drawing a few times before you go freehand. Tracing isn't cheating—it's just another way to practice!

SQUIRTLE

Squirtle's shell provides protection during battle, but this little Pokémon also fights back with winning Water-type moves. Once you learn how to draw Squirtle, you can use your winning moves to take on its more evolved forms: Wartortle, Blastoise, and Mega Blastoise.

1 The guidelines in this drawing are slanted. That's because Squirtle is leaning to the side, ready for action. Use the angled guidelines to sketch in the basic shapes of Squirtle's body and a curlicue for the tail.

2 Squirtle's right leg sticks straight out, but the left leg is bent. Position the arms at an angle next to Squirtle's head. If you squint your eyes, the whole body should look like the letter X.

3 Detail time! Finish off the tail and shell with curved lines. Then draw two curved lines inside the mouth for the tongue and use zigzags for the fingers and toes. Study the different shapes inside the eyes before you draw them. For the pattern on Squirtle's tummy, start with a star, and then erase the pointy tips.

4 Almost done! Erase any lines that are getting in the way. Does Squirtle look like it's ready to unleash a Rain Dance? Try drawing a burst of water blasting out of Squirtle's mouth, or some match-winning bubbles!

CHARMANDER

Get out your reds, oranges, and yellows! The glowing flame on the tip of this Fire type's tail shows that Charmander is in great shape. Are you in great shape for drawing? Warm up by scribbling basic shapes and lines on scrap paper.

1 Use this step to set up the entire drawing. How big is the head compared to the body? Where does the tail connect to the body? Don't worry about how your drawing looks at this stage. Just get down the basics.

2 Take a good look at Charmander's face. The eyes are set as wide as this Fire-type's smile. Now draw the outline of a flame on the tip of Charmander's tail.

3 Take a minute to reshape the outline of Charmander's body. If you get confused, look at the final drawing to guide you. Then add details like teeth, eyes, claws, and more flames. Don't forget to add the curve of Charmander's belly!

4 Erase extra lines and smudges. Now stand back and compare your drawing to the one in the book. Is anything missing? Does one leg look like it's in front of the body while the other is behind it? If not, make sure you erased the right lines.

BULBASAUR

Bulbasaur uses the big seed bulb on its back to soak up nutrients from the sun. This Grass- and Poison-type Pokémon has powerful moves. Are you ready to show off your mighty drawing moves? Then let's take on Bulbasaur!

1 Start by breaking this drawing down into the simplest shapes. For Bulbasaur, that's a big, boxy head and half an oval for the body.

2 Draw a squished-heart shape for the mouth. Then add loose triangles for the eyes. Now sketch in the seed on Bulbasaur's back and three chubby legs. The lines for the legs closest to you go up and over the body. The lines for the leg farthest away from you are hidden behind the body.

3

Add details like spots on the skin and tiny triangles for the teeth and toenails. Inside each eye, draw a curved line next to an oval. Then add curves to the bulb on Bulbasaur's back.

4

Erase the guidelines you drew in step one, and make any final corrections. Now that you know how to draw Bulbasaur, try drawing it in action. Add vines popping out of the seed on its back for Vine Whip!

MEOWTH

Uh-oh! Team Rocket's Meowth looks like he's scared of something. Maybe he just heard that Jessie and James are out of food again. Knowing Meowth, he will do whatever it takes to get something yummy in his tummy.

1 Start with a sideways oval for Meowth's head. Add a body, arms, legs, hands, and feet. Meowth's ears are shaped like rounded triangles. Don't forget the jewel in the center of his head. It is shaped like a rectangle with rounded corners.

2 Now give Meowth a tail. Notice how the tail starts where Meowth's body and legs meet. Round out the shape of Meowth's hands and feet. Then draw whiskers on the sides and top of his head—six whiskers in all.

3 Give Meowth some toes and fingers on his paws and erase any extra lines. Add detail to the jewel and tail. Finally, give Meowth a wavy line for a mouth. Make sure it is curved down to give it a worried look.

4 Draw two pointy triangle teeth, then sketch in the eyes. As you can see, they are not perfect circles, but more like rounded diamonds.

5 Finish up Meowth by adding details to his eyes. Color in the black part on his ears. You've drawn Meowth—that's right!

GENGAR

This Ghost- and Poison-type Pokémon has a devious sense of humor. If you hear shadows laughing on the night of a full moon, chances are a Gengar is haunting you! A face-off with Gengar can be bone-chilling. Luckily, this drawing doesn't have to be scary. Making mistakes is a great way to practice and learn how to get better!

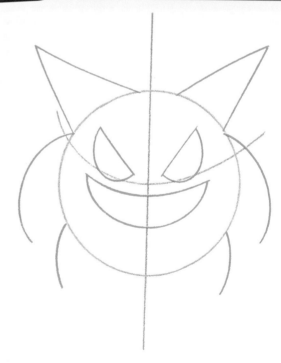

DRAWING TIP
The next few drawings all start with circles, so practice drawing them on scrap paper before you dive in!

1 Start with two guidelines and a circle. The horizontal guideline is curved like a U. It will help you draw Gengar's ghoulish grin!

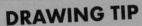

2 Decision time! Where do you want to draw the triangular ears? Where will the arms and legs go? Where will you place the half-moons that will become the eyes and mouth?

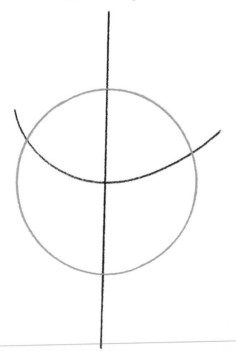

3 Time to start adding details! Draw the teeth and eyes. Then use lots of pointed curved lines for Gengar's fingers, toes, and ghostly spikes.

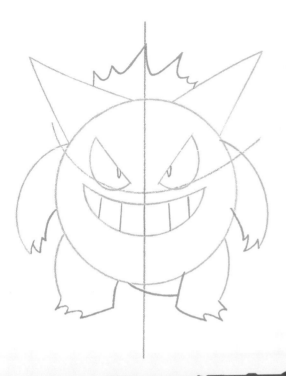

4 Check to see if any lines or shapes are missing. Then erase the guidelines and starter shapes. You're almost done!

5 This Shadow Pokémon has a purple body and red eyes. You can use a straight purple marker or crayon to color the body, or experiment with layers of red and blue colored pencils to come up with your own poisonous purple.

DRAWING TIP

Want your circle to be crisp and clean? Try tracing around the bottom of a round cup!

WOOLOO

Wooloo roam in the wild of the Galar region. Have you noticed that the body of this Sheep Pokémon is shaped kind of like a cloud? That's because it's covered in curly fleece that is SO FLUFFY, Wooloo could fall off a cliff and not get hurt. Drawing this Pokémon can help you feel just as safe and cozy along your drawing journey!

1 Start by drawing a circle. Then draw a curved line in the upper left-hand corner. This will be your guideline. Wooloo's whole face will fit on the left side of it!

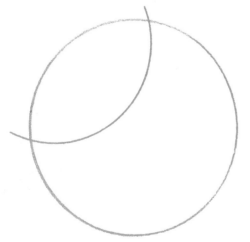

2 Lightly sketch a vertical guideline on the face to show where the eye and horn will be. Then use curved lines to outline the face. Finally, sketch in the basic shapes of the legs and tail.

DRAWING TIP
Keep the lines in the first two steps light and loose so they are easier to go over as you refine your drawing.

3 Ready to start adding details? Draw the oval-shaped eye and triangular horn. Then use curved lines to sketch the ears, the rest of the legs, and Wooloo's long braid.

4 Stick with it! This step is all about details! Use the same kind of line you'd use to draw a cloud to draw the curly fleece on Wooloo's body. Then add details in the ears, eyes, and hair.

COUNTING SHEEP

How many Wooloo can you draw on one sheet of paper? Draw them, then count them. But don't fall asleep!

5 Erase any lines you don't need. How does your Wooloo look? Make any needed changes to the outline and get ready for color! How many different shades of gray do you see on Wooloo's body? What will you use to color it in?

ROOKIDEE

This Flying-type Pokémon may be small, but it's also super brave. Rookidee will take on any opponent no matter how big or powerful, and it never seems to get weaker—even when it doesn't win. That's because Rookidee sees every battle as a chance to learn and get stronger—win or lose. Think of this drawing as a chance to learn and see how it goes!

1 Start by drawing a big circle. Then add a straight horizontal line near the top of the circle where you think the eyes should go. Use a ruler or straightedge if you like. Then add a smaller circle under that line and off to the right. Can you imagine what part of Rookidee it will become?

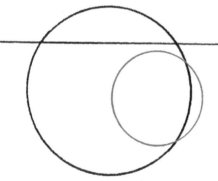

2 Sketch some feathers to the right of the smaller circle. Is it starting to look like a wing? Then it's time to make some choices! Where will the eye go? Draw a U shape. Where will the feet go? Draw four dashes to get them started. What about the top feathers? Try using zigzags!

DRAWING TIP
Keep the lines in the first two steps light and loose so they are easier to go over as you refine your drawing.

3 Now take a step back. Does your drawing look like a Rookidee? Add a few more details to connect the lines and shapes you drew in step two. Use two ovals to finish off the eye and draw a tail feather below the wing. What kinds of lines will you use for the pattern on Rookidee's chest and the feathers on its head?

LOOK CLOSER
Work out those drawing muscles! Practice makes better! Trace Rookidee's claws on scrap paper to get a feel for the shapes. Then try them freehand on scrap paper a few times before adding them to your drawing.

4 Use an eraser to clean up your drawing. Which lines will stay? Which lines will go? Did you notice that part of the guideline became the bottom of the eye? Can you still see the circle you started out with for the body?

5 Time for color! Rookidee is a beautiful blue-and-yellow bird. Will you use markers, crayons, or watercolors to brighten up this Tiny Bird Pokémon?

TOGEDEMARU

Togedemaru has long, spiny fur that bristles during storms to attract lightning. Warm up your drawing arm by sketching lightning-fast circles on scrap paper. Sometimes, the faster you draw a circle, the less you worry, and the rounder it turns out!

1 Start by sketching a big circle. Draw with your whole arm, not just your wrist. And remember, it doesn't have to be perfect! Now divide the circle into four parts with two quick guidelines.

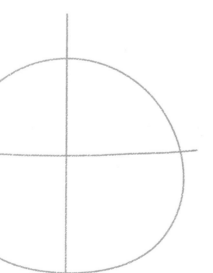

2 Use the guidelines to help you place the eyes, ears, feet, and cheeks. Did you notice that the tips of the ears peek out above the original circle? Use a zigzag and a curved line to draw the tail above the right ear.

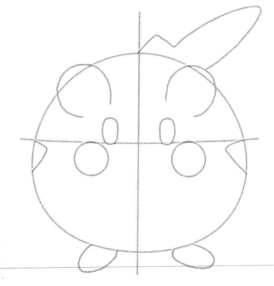

3 Do you like where you've placed all the features? Great! Then add details like the eyes, nose, and mouth. And use V-shaped lines around the edges of the circle to show off Togedemaru's spiky fur.

4 You got this! Erase the original guideline and any other lines you don't need. Would you like to change or adjust anything? If not, it's time to color! Togedemaru's cheeks are yellow, but most of its body is gray and white.

ELDEGOSS

This drawing starts with a BIG circle that will become the cotton fluff on top of Eldegoss's head. Eldegoss uses the cotton as a cushion to protect its head from attacks, but it can also be spun into beautiful, glossy yarn—a Galar region specialty! Trace around the base of a cup or draw the circle freehand. The choice is yours!

1 Start by drawing two guidelines that lean to the right and—you guessed it!—a big circle. Leave lots of space above the horizontal guideline to make the cotton fluff look huge compared to the rest of the body!

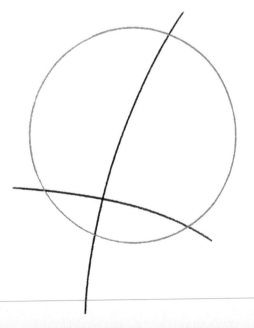

2 Now draw the face. For Eldegoss, start by drawing a small circle at the spot where the guidelines cross. Then draw the eyes right on the horizontal guideline. Finish off with some detail on the forehead and a small, smiling mouth. Then add the basic shapes of the upper body.

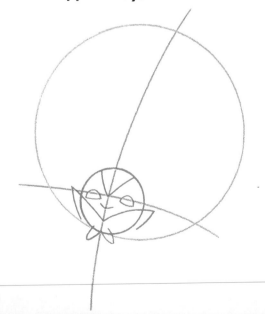

3 Now sketch the flowing shapes of the lower body and crown. Don't forget to draw the seeds in Eldegoss's fluff. They're full of nutrients! When Eldegoss spreads them on the wind, all Galarian Pokémon benefit!

LOOK CLOSER
Remember, you can always look back at the introduction of this book for tips on drawing faces.

4 Use tiny hatch marks to add texture to the cotton fluff. Isn't it cool that you can draw how something feels?

5 Erase the guidelines and starter shapes. Eldegoss's cotton fluff should be all hatch marks now. How does your drawing look? Do you need to refine any of your marks before you trace over them with a thin black marker? This Grass-type Pokémon's body is a beautiful shade of yellow-green. When you're coloring, try adding a curved shadow at the base of the cotton fluff to make Eldegoss look three-dimensional!

BOUNSWEET

Mallow's Bounsweet loves to race Ash's Pikachu across the sand. But you don't have to race to finish this drawing. Take your time and practice any challenging shapes on scrap paper before adding them to your final piece.

1 Start with a big circle for the body. Then add two smaller ovals to the top for leaves. Now sketch in a quick, curved guideline. Make sure it's a little off-center for a three-quarter view.

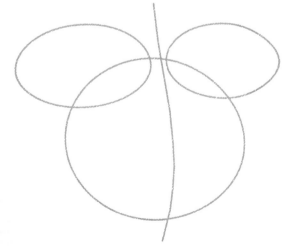

2 Connect the leaves with a smaller oval. Then draw two tiny ovals for the eyes. Using curved lines, sketch in the basic cloud shape at the bottom of Bounsweet's body. Now draw a V shape below the circle for the tail.

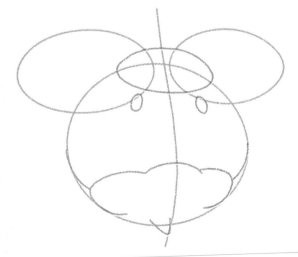

3 Time to add details—like a sweet smile! Draw a curvy stem at the top of the head. Then sketch details on the leaves and body. Now do a check. Are all the lines where you want them to be? Suh-WEET!

4 Erase any smudges and extra lines. Ready for a color explosion? Bounsweet's leafy cap is bright green, and most of its body is a rich berry or fuchsia. Let the white of the paper show through for the frilly band at the bottom.

APPLIN

Applin is a Dragon- and Grass-type Pokémon with an excellent strategy. How does a small, wormlike Pokémon avoid bigger Bird Pokémon? As soon as it is born, Applin burrows into an apple and uses it as protection and a food source until it evolves! Sweet! What snacks get you geared up to take your drawing to the next level?

1 Applin's body is round, but the starter shape is an upside-down teardrop instead of a circle. If it's easier, you can turn your paper upside down and draw the teardrop right-side up! Did you notice that the whole starter shape sits below the horizontal guideline?

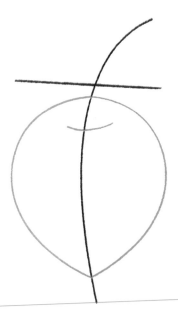

2 The leaves at the top of this drawing look kind of like a heart. Try drawing one half and then the other. Draw a half circle outside the bottom of the teardrop. This will become the dragon worm in the next step. Use a combination of curved and jagged lines for the details at the bottom of the body.

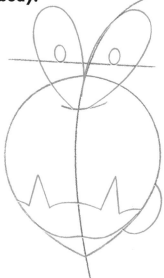

DRAWING TIP
Not sure where a line is supposed to be? Take a look at the finished drawing to help you understand that line's job in the drawing.

3 Now use curved lines to add details at the top of the body. Then take a closer look at the dragon. How would you break this up into lines and shapes to make it easier to draw?

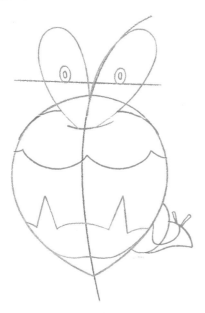

4 Erase all guidelines and smudges. Then take a good look at your drawing. Are there any tweaks to be made? Does the outline of Applin's body look more like an apple? Once you've made all the adjustments, trace over the outlines with a thin black marker.

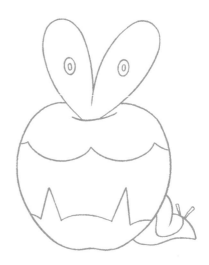

 DID YOU KNOW?

Applin that live in tart apples evolve into Flapple. And Applin that live in sweet apples evolve into Appletun. What's the story of your Applin's Evolution? Draw it here!

PANCHAM

For a small Pokémon, Pancham has big moves! You have big decisions to make before you start to draw. Will your drawing of Pancham take up the whole paper? Or will it leap off the page?

1 Decide where to place Pancham on the paper. Then lightly sketch in guidelines and some basic shapes. The vertical guideline is slanted to give a sense of motion.

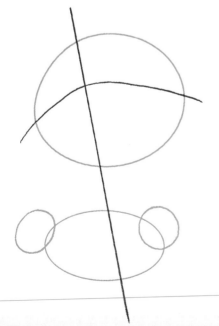

2 Use the guidelines to help you position the shapes in the face. Then connect the head to the body with a big, upside-down U. Next, draw the arms on an angle. The right arm looks shorter than the left because it's farther away.

3 Clean up the outline of Pancham's body. Then start at the top and add details like a zigzag of hair, ovals inside the eyes, and another zigzag for the teeth. Don't forget to draw a leafy sprig next to the mouth. This leaf helps Pancham track its opponents' movements.

4 Do you need to make any changes to your drawing? Does Pancham look like it's leaping into the air? If not, maybe its bottom paws are not high enough. When you're ready, get out your colors. Here's a tip: Use a darker color for the inside of the mouth than for the tongue.

SNORLAX

Shake it up to wake it up! You won't start with a circle for this drawing. Instead, you'll get to play around with big sweeping curves and perspective! That's because Snorlax is known as the Sleeping Pokémon, and it's almost always lying down—so its feet are closer to you than its head! Try taping a giant piece of paper to the wall so you can draw an extra-large Snorlax. You'll have to move your whole body as you draw!

1 The vertical guideline for Snorlax is straight. But the horizontal guideline is a big, upside-down U shape. Draw them both. Then sketch a circle for each foot and two curved lines for the face. Remember, the feet are bigger than the face because they are closer to you.

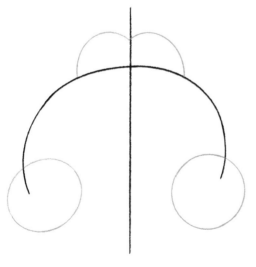

2 This drawing shows a rare moment when Snorlax is awake and waving. Use light curved lines to place the arms. Then sketch in the outline of the ears and the pads on the bottoms of Snorlax's feet.

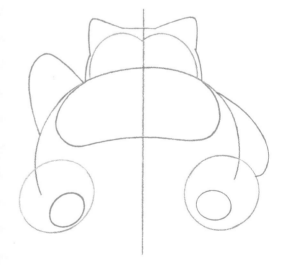

3

It's time to add details like the face and nails. The fingernails are basic zigzags, but the toes are cones. Add a curved line to the bottom of a triangle to make it look three-dimensional!

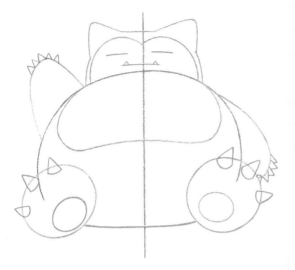

LOOK CLOSER

To draw a cone that looks 3-D, start with an oval. Then draw a triangle on top of it. Erase the dotted line and you have a Snorlax toe!

Did you know?

The average Snorlax starts at about 1,000 pounds. But in Galar, Snorlax can Gigantamax and grow to many times their original size! A Pokémon that big can stop a speeding train in its tracks!

4

Now take a step back and evaluate your drawing. What does it need? What can you erase? Did you remember to add the line for the bottom of the body?

MUNCHLAX

Happy to be hungry? This hyper little Pokémon loves to chow down. All. The. Time! Munchlax will do anything for food, like rummage through garbage cans, run for miles, or even stop in the middle of a Pokémon battle! Munchlax isn't as big—or as sleepy—as its evolved form, Snorlax, but you'll still need plenty of big circles and sweeping curves to draw this Pokémon.

1 Start with guidelines as usual. Then draw a big circle for the body. Finish up by adding a shape that looks like a football for the head and ovals for the hands and feet.

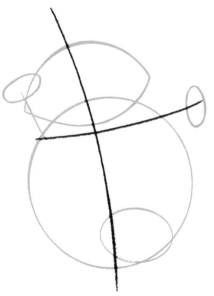

2 Take it slow. Start with the easier parts like the zigzags on the fingers and body. Then work on the head. Draw the jaw jutting out from the football shape you drew in step one. Then add a wide U to show the inside of the mouth. Finally, draw two ovals for eyes.

Lighten up! Keep your grip loose and move your entire arm as you draw—not just your wrist.

Think big! Start out with the big shapes. Save the details for the end.

3 Way to go! The hardest parts of the drawing are already done. Add details like upside-down V shapes for the ears, teeth, and toes. Then erase any lines you don't need.

4 Stop and take a step back from your drawing. You might even want to tape it up to the wall. Sitting too close makes it harder to spot things that need to be fixed.

Feeling as hungry as Munchlax? Healthy snacks like carrot sticks and nuts can help you stay energized and focused while drawing.

5 Now take out your markers and get ready to color!

MORPEKO

Do you like to draw as much as Morpeko likes to eat? This Electric-type Pokémon chews the seeds stored in its pocket-like pouches to create electricity. But when it gets too hungry, watch out! This Two-Sided Pokémon goes from sweet to hangry. How can you use color to show the two sides of Morpeko's personality?

1 Start with two guidelines and—you guessed it!—a circle for the head. Make sure the spot where the guidelines cross is not in the center of the circle. The horizontal guideline curves because Morpeko's face isn't flat.

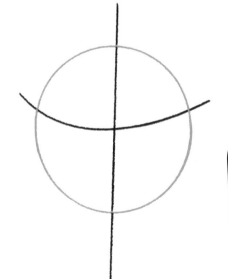

Check out Morpeko's cheeks! Do you notice any similarities to the drawing you made of Pikachu? What's the same? What's different?

2 Sketch in the circles for Morpeko's eyes and cheeks. Use curved lines to draw the arm and ears. Then draw a straight line on the lower body that will become Morpeko's pocket-like pouches.

42

3 Continue adding basic shapes—a dot for the nose, and more curves on the head, arms, feet, and mouth. Keep your lines light and loose so you can erase them later. Don't forget to draw a circle in the hand. Morpeko is never without seeds, and neither is this drawing!

4 Zig your zag! Remember those zigzags you practiced in the warm-up challenge? Draw them here to set off each side of Morpeko's body. Then add the rest of the details to the face and body.

SHOCKING

Have you noticed that many Electric-type Pokémon like Morpeko, Pikachu, and Charjabug use zigzag lines to show off their charged nature? How many other Pokémon with zigzags have you found in this book? Are they all Electric types?

5 Now take a good look at your Morpeko. Are all the lines where you want them to be? Did you sketch the curved lines inside the mouth for the tooth and tongue? Great! Erase any lines you don't need and fix any lines that need fixing.

DRAWING CHALLENGE

Now that you can draw Morpeko, try drawing Morpeko in Hangry Mode! The eyes are red half-moons like Gengar's, and the body is purple and gray!

BEWEAR

This super-strong Pokémon has big arms that are great for giving bone-crushing bear hugs. And this drawing of Bewear is made of big shapes, so loosen up your drawing arm by drawing jellybeans, circles, and rectangles on a big piece of scrap paper. Remember to move your whole arm as you draw, not just your wrist!

1 Start by drawing a circle on top of a rectangle with rounded corners. Make sure they overlap a tiny bit. Then quickly sketch in two crisscrossed guidelines. The horizontal guideline should be curved to help you draw Bewear's face in the next step.

2 Use the guidelines to place Bewear's eyes and football-shaped snout. Draw two ears outside the top half of the circle. Then use big, sweeping movements to sketch in the arms and legs.

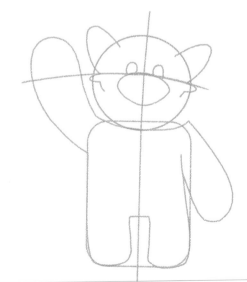

3 Most of the details in the paws and face are circles and ovals. Take some extra time to sketch the curved lines that make up Bewear's tail. They'll help your drawing begin to look 3-D.

4 Add color, like a bubblegum pink head and paw pads. When you're finished, you can trace over the outlines with a thin black marker.

DRAWING TIP:

Try drawing this Bewear catching Team Rocket or sending them off with a new blast!

CHARJABUG

Charjabug is the evolved form of Grubbin. Do you feel like you're already turning into a Pokémon champion artist? Let's find out! The starting shape for Charjabug's body isn't a circle this time. It's a 3-D box. Thinking in 3-D while you draw helps create depth and volume in your artwork. And it makes your drawing look more lifelike!

1 Start by sketching a 3-D box. Keep your lines light and loose in case you have to erase them. Sound hard? You can always practice on scrap paper before you begin!

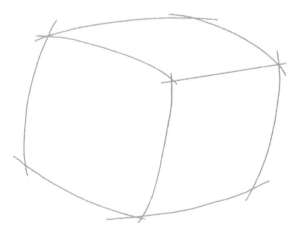

2 The decorative lines that wrap around Charjabug's body are curved, not straight. So are the triangles' lines on the bottom right-hand side of the body. Now draw two rounded cones on the front of the box for Charjabug's pincers.

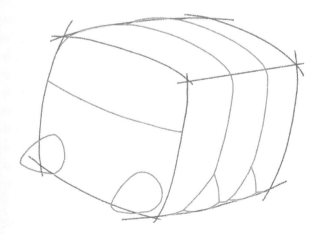

3 Ready for an electrifying secret? All the details in this drawing are simple lines and shapes. There's a vertical zigzag on the front of the body along with six straight lines. And don't forget the two ovals on the side!

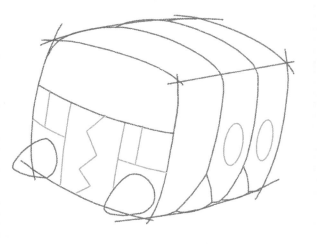

4 Time to clean up your drawing! Try molding a rubber eraser into a point to get inside the edges and corners. Are there any lines or angles that need to be redrawn? Fix them now. Then get ready to color!

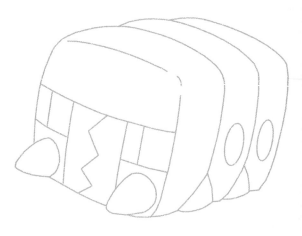

EISCUE

This Penguin Pokémon knows how to chill out! To keep from overheating, Eiscue keeps its head in a block of ice! Remember that cube you learned to draw for Charjabug's body? You'll get to use it here for the head. Need a refresher? Here's a breakdown of how to draw a cube. How well do you think in 3-D?

Thinking in 3-D helps create an illusion of depth and volume in your artwork. It makes your final drawing look more convincing.

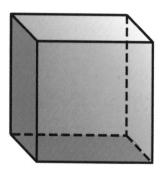

1 Start with slightly curved guidelines. Then draw an oval for the body on the bottom half of the vertical guideline. Make sure it doesn't touch the horizontal guideline at all.

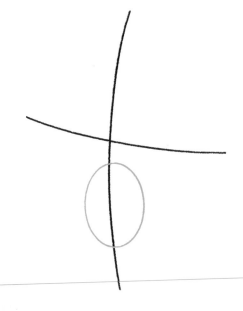

2 Draw a cube to shape Eiscue's frosty head. Make sure it overlaps the oval body and looks like it's covering the neck. Then place two ovals for eyes on top of the horizontal guideline. Finally, sketch in the basic shapes of the flippers and feet!

3 Don't get derailed! Add details! Draw a curved line on the left edge of each eye to make it look like it's been carved out of the ice. Then sketch in a diamond for the beak and use zigzags for the toes and tail. Remember to use the guidelines to help get the placement right.

4 Erase any lines you don't need and take a minute to smooth out any outlines or details. Then use shades of blue and gray to put a sheen on this Penguin Pokémon. Did you remember to draw the single hair on Eiscue's head? Eiscue dangles that hair in water to catch fish!

GALARIAN DARUMAKA

Ice is nice! Outside Galar, Darumaka are Fire types that get their power—and energy—from the fires burning inside their bodies. But in Galar, Darumaka have lived in snowy areas for so long that their fire sacs cooled off! The colder Darumaka get, the more energetic they become! What gives you the most energy to draw?

1 This Galarian Darumaka will be dancing on one leg, so use guidelines that lean to the right. Then lightly sketch a potato shape for the body.

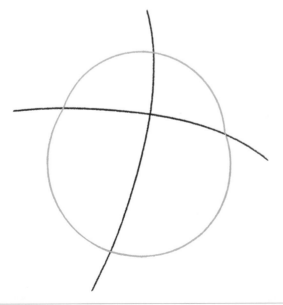

2 Use this step to set up the basics. Sketch half circles for the legs and arms, ovals for the eyes, and diamonds for the ice crystals on Darumaka's chest.

3

Now pause and take a careful look at the drawing in the book. Have you captured all the details? Sketch in hands and feet and don't forget the curves around the eyes.

TWICE IS NICE

Trace over the shapes of the ice crystals above Darumaka's eyes a few times on scrap paper before trying them freehand. How would you break them down into basic shapes?

4

That potato starter shape was helpful for sketching in all the basics, but it's not the true shape of Darumaka's body. Refine the outline of Darumaka's body, then erase any lines you don't need. Now take a step back. What did you like most about making this drawing?

BLIPBUG

This Bug-type Pokémon is often found in gardens and loves to collect information. Just like Applin and Grubbin, it's a tiny Pokémon that has to avoid bigger Bird Pokémon like Rookidee! Can you tell this Blipbug is super smart just by looking at it? What visual clues in the drawing tipped you off? Have fun drawing all the ovals and big sweeping curves that make up this Pokémon!

1 Start with a long oval for the head. Then draw an angled guideline at the very bottom. The vertical guideline in this drawing looks like a backward J. It will help you set up the shape of Blipbug's body.

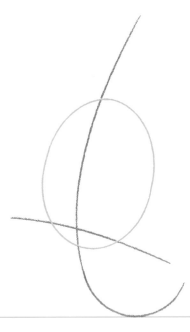

2 Draw two more long ovals for the eyes. Lightly sketch in a collar at the base of the neck and attach a jellybean shape for the body. Go ahead and draw two circles on the body for a foot and arm. Then sketch in the basic details on the head.

3 This step uses mostly curved lines to add details. Do you see the similarity between the shapes of the bow-tie feelers, tail, and head details? Use U shapes to tuck the back legs behind the body.

4 Many of the lines in this step—like the ones in the eyes and on Blipbug's head—show you where to put different colors. So, clean up your lines and get out your crayons, markers, or paints! What colors will you need to finish up this drawing?

DRAWING CHALLENGE
Blipbug's happy place is a garden. What's your happy place? Draw yourself hanging out with your favorite Pokémon there!

DRAWING TIP
If you're having a hard time with a drawing, take a break! Try doing something else or drawing an easier Pokémon. Then come back to the more complicated drawing later on when you're feeling less frustrated!

YAMPER

These Electric-type Pokémon crackle with energy when they run, so watch out! When they get too excited, they may give you a shock! Like most Puppy Pokémon, Yamper have a very important job—to love and protect their Trainers! Do you need a challenge? Try drawing this playful pup. Then give yourself a treat!

1 Start this drawing with two curved guidelines and a circle for the head. You can also add a horizontal guideline to the face where the eyes will go. Remember to keep it curved! Then draw the basic shape of Yamper's body.

2 Draw the nose on the vertical guideline and the oval eyes on the horizontal guideline. You can make the far eye look farther away by drawing it a little smaller than the eye that's closest to you. Now add in more basic shapes for the ears, legs, tail, and neck fluff.

3 Use different kinds of curved lines for details like the bow of the mouth and the shape inside the ear. Then draw a teardrop behind the tail shape. You'll refine it in the next step.

4 Use this step to clean up your drawing and to rework the shape of the face and body. Erase the extra lines in Yamper's tail. Does it look like a little lightning bolt?

LOOK CLOSER

SOBBLE

These Water Lizard Pokémon are the perfect partners for a journey through the Galar region. Sobble are sensitive and caring. When a Sobble cries, its opponents cry, too! Sobble can also change colors when they get wet to blend into their environments. So, if you have to erase part of your drawing, you can always just say the first Sobble turned invisible!

1 Start off as usual with two guidelines and two starter shapes. Make sure the horizontal guideline turns down at the ends to match Sobble's mood.

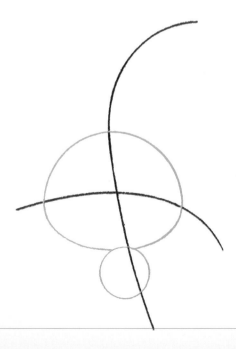

2 Sketch in the facial features and the body. Use ovals to start blocking in the tail. There's a lot going on in this step, so take your time and break it down. Remember to start simple and get more specific in step three.

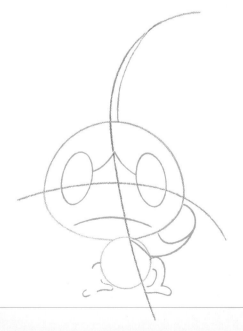

3 Add arms and connect the ovals you drew for the tail to the body with a long sweeping line. Then focus on the face. Sobble has a blue oval on each cheek and three ovals in each eye! When you're done, lightly sketch in the fin on its head.

4 Did you keep your lines light and loose in steps one to three? Good! Now's the time to choose which lines will stay and which will go. Do any of the marks need a touch-up before you finalize the outline with marker?

Did you know?
You can block in colors the same way you block in the basic lines and shapes of a Pokémon. Loosely block in the basic colors. Then add details and shading to make Sobble look more three-dimensional!

GROOKEY

Want to start your journey through Galar with a Grass-type Pokémon that will keep you grooving as you go? Then Grookey is your Pokémon! Grookey drums a special stick to create sound waves that help the plants and flowers grow. Cool! But watch out, because Grookey also drums when it's about to attack. The faster the beat, the more pumped it is for battle!

1 Draw your guidelines. One is straight and the other is slanted. Then draw a half-circle right on top of that horizontal guideline. Follow up with a slanted oval for the body.

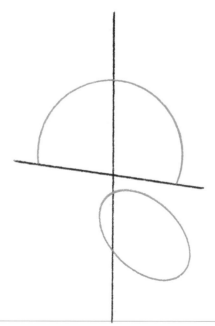

2 Attach the head to the body oval with curved lines. Then use ovals for the eyes and mouth area. When you're ready, sketch in the basic shapes of the arms and the leaves on top of Grookey's head.

3

Start adding the details that will get this Grookey grooving, like the stick on its head and the curved tail on its bottom. Take a minute to connect the legs to the body and to add details in the eyes, nose, and mouth.

4

Add more details like the pattern around Grooky's eyes and the details in the ears, leaves, and legs. Are you already thinking about the colors you'll use to make this Pokémon pop?

LOOK CLOSER

Feeling stumped by the legs? Break it down! Try tracing them on scrap paper a few times to get a feel for where the lines go.

5

Take a step back so see if any of your lines needs adjusting or erasing before you add color. Now that you can draw Grookey, imagine it battling Pokémon in the wild areas of the Galar region. What moves will it use? What Pokémon will it help you catch?

SCORBUNNY

All fired up to explore the Galar region? Then you might want to choose this Fire-type Pokémon to join you on your journey. Scorbunny is always ready for battle! It warms up by running around in circles to get its fire energy pumping. Are you pumped to draw? Warm up by making big circles with your arms. Then practice drawing ovals on a piece of scrap paper. Can you feel the heat?

1 This is a really active pose, so start with two quick curved guidelines. Then draw an oval for the head where the guidelines cross. Draw a smaller oval for the body that touches the first oval. Then sketch in two quick curved lines for the ears.

2 Place the facial features. Then focus on the shapes of the arms and feet. They look a little like jellybeans. Make sure one foot overlaps the left arm. When you're done, sketch in the outline of the ears—they're kind of like rounded zigzags.

DRAWING TIP
Go with your gut! Sometimes the faster you draw a line or shape, the less you stress!

3 Use short curved lines to separate the toes and fingers. Then draw the details in the eyes, mouth, and ears. See those rectangular pads on Scorbunny's forehead and foot? They get super hot when Scorbunny is ready to fight!

4 Erase the guidelines so you can get a good look at all the details. Did you catch the collar around Scorbunny's neck and the way the nose connects to the rest of the face? If you're happy with all your outlines, go ahead and trace over them with a marker. You're on fire!

DRAWING CHALLENGE
Now that you can draw Scorbunny, try drawing this Fire-type Pokémon in action! Is it Double Kicking a snoozing Snorlax, evolving into Raboot, or helping its Trainer catch even more Pokémon? The choice is yours!

GALARIAN STUNFISK

Unlike the Stunfisk found in other regions, Galarian Stunfisk have mouths shaped like Poké Balls. These Trap Pokémon hang out with their mouths open until other Pokémon come along and then—SNAP! The challenge of this drawing is that Galarian Stunfisk's face is on its back—so you'll have lots of opportunities to practice perspective.

1 Start with two guidelines. Then draw a jellybean shape around them. Having trouble getting the perspective right? Try tracing the guidelines and drawing the jellybean freehand!

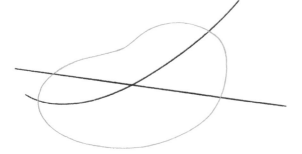

2 Draw zigzags at the front and back of the jellybean. Then draw three ovals along the horizontal guideline. Finally, sketch in the basic shapes of the fins. Notice how the fin that's farther away is much smaller and mostly hidden by the body.

3 There are a lot of details in this step, so take your time. Use curved lines to define the fins. Then tackle the pattern on Stunfisk's back.

4 Clean up your drawing and trace over the final outlines with black marker. What colors will you use for the Poké Ball mouth? What colors will you use on the body to show off the distinct pattern on Galarian Stunfisk's back?

LOOK CLOSER
How would you break the mouth down into basic shapes?

DRAWING CHALLENGE
Now that you can draw a Galarian Stunfisk, try drawing this Ground- and Steel-type Pokémon luring another Pokémon into its trap!

ARROKUDA

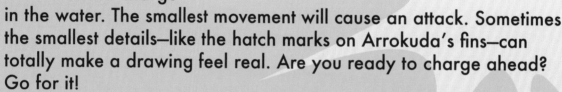

Good luck escaping this Water-type Pokémon's sharp, pointed jaw! Arrokuda uses its fins to charge in the water. The smallest movement will cause an attack. Sometimes the smallest details—like the hatch marks on Arrokuda's fins—can totally make a drawing feel real. Are you ready to charge ahead? Go for it!

1 Unlike the other Pokémon in this book, Arrokuda are long and lean. So, start with two guidelines and a simple curve for the back.

2 Attack this step by nailing down the shape of the sharp, pointed jaw. Then get ready to use lots of curved lines as you sketch in the rest of the body, fins, and circular eye. Notice that the whole face sits to the right of the vertical guideline and that the fins look like a folded heart.

3 There are a lot of details to add in this step—like the rest of the fins and the cool pattern on Arrokuda's side. Use the horizontal guideline as the center of each arrowhead shape. Remember, the shapes get smaller as they get closer to the tail.

4 Erase the guidelines and add your finishing touches! What colors will you use to finish off this proud piece? Make sure to choose a bright, poppy orange for the fin at the base of the neck.

Arrokuda get sluggish when they eat too much. Feeling sluggish from drawing so much? Take a break!

CHEWTLE

This Snapping Pokémon has a massive mandible! So, loosen up your drawing arm and get ready to use lots of curves and ovals! Like its evolved form, Drednaw, Chewtle starts off battles by butting opponents with its rock-solid horn. But then Chewtle bites down and never lets go! Are you ready to draw with as much determination as this Water-type Pokémon? Snap to it!

1 Start with two guidelines. Chewtle's jaw is the most distinctive—and crushing—part of its body. So, set up the head with a big sweeping curve that stretches from one end of the horizontal guideline to the other. Then add an oval for the body.

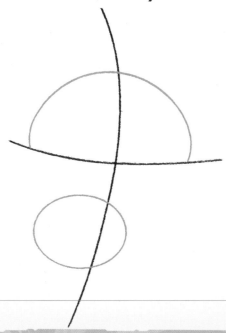

2 Draw a circle for the cheek. Then it's all curves from here! The brow, the details on the body, and even the rock-hard horn Chewtle uses to attack opponents are all curved lines. See how the wavy mouth sits right on the horizontal guideline?

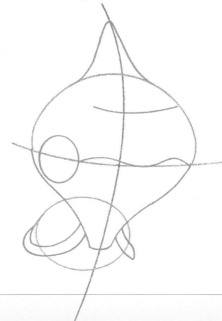

3

Use smaller ovals for the eyes. Make the mouth shape even more dramatic by adding a U shape to the middle. Finish up with the basic shapes of the tail and legs.

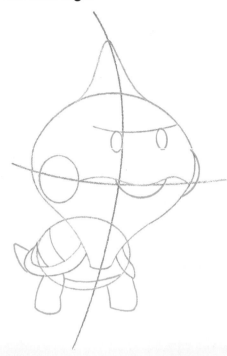

LOOK CLOSER

Look at the way the curved lines in the body overlap one another. Practice on scrap paper or dive right in!

5

Get rid of any lines you don't need. Now turn your drawing upside down. Sometimes changing your perspective helps you spot lines or details that need to be changed—or celebrated!

4

Add details in the eyes, nose, and toes. See how the back legs are smaller and tucked behind the body? That helps show perspective.

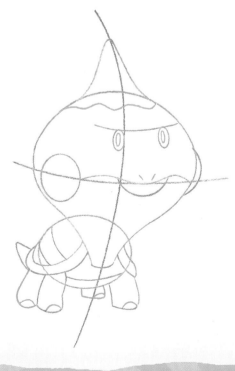

DRAWING TIP

Chewtle's head is so big, it casts the rest of its body into shadow. When you're coloring in this Water-type Pokémon, shade the bottom of the head and body with a warmer tone to show off the shadows.

CUFANT

This super-cute Steel-type Pokémon is also super strong. It uses the elliptical end of its trunk to dig in the ground and its round body to carry more than five tons of weight with no problem at all. Thankfully, you don't need to do any heavy lifting for this drawing. Try drawing this Cufant freehand before you go back and break it down. Have fun with it!

1 Start with two curved guidelines. Then sketch in the basic shape of the body and the shovel tip of Cufant's trunk.

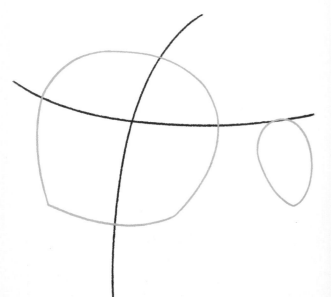

2 Connect the tip of the trunk to the body with curved lines. Add the two closer legs. Draw a half circle for the far ear and an oval for the eye. Keep building up the basic shapes until you have something that looks roughly like an elephant.

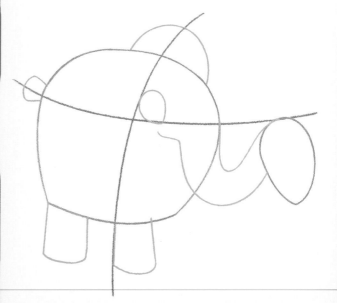

3

Sketch in the front ear—it looks kind of like a heart! Then start adding details like the pattern on Cufant's head and trunk.

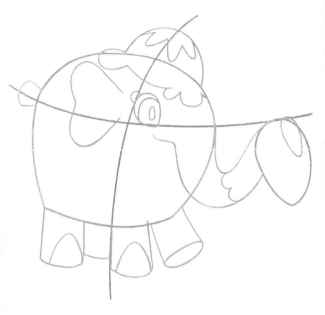

LOOK CLOSER

Cufant's raised leg is a cylinder—a three-dimensional tube shape. And it's simpler to draw than it looks! Start by drawing an oval for the bottom of the foot. Then connect the oval to the body with two slightly curved lines.

4

Have fun decorating Cufant with curved lines and ovals! Then clean up your drawing and trace over the outlines with a marker.

5

Erase any lines you don't need. Cufant's body is coated in copper—and turns green when it rains! What colors will you use to make the pattern pop on Cufant's trunk?

DRAWING CHALLENGE

Play around! Pokémon aren't perfect—and neither is art! Pick a Pokémon and try drawing it with your nondominant hand. Or draw Pikachu with your eyes closed. Have fun with each new challenge!

CLOBBOPUS

This Fighting-type Pokémon is also known as the Tantrum Pokémon. It's very curious, but it checks things out by clobbering them with its tentacles! Are you curious about the lines and shapes you'll use to build this drawing? Here's a tip: Take a look at the final drawing first. What basic shapes do you think you'll use? What kinds of lines will you need for all the details?

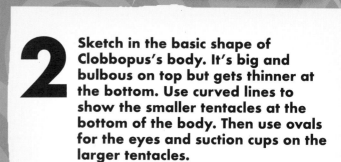

1 This drawing starts out in a similar way to Chewtle—with two guidelines and a big sweeping curve for the top of the head. Once you've sketched those, draw an oval for the end of each thumping tentacle.

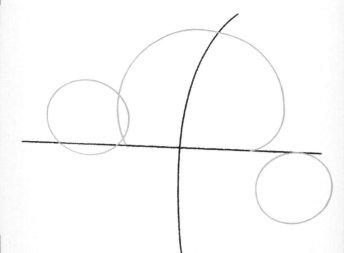

2 Sketch in the basic shape of Clobbopus's body. It's big and bulbous on top but gets thinner at the bottom. Use curved lines to show the smaller tentacles at the bottom of the body. Then use ovals for the eyes and suction cups on the larger tentacles.

3 Use more ovals to draw the pattern on Clobbopus's head, the suction cups on its tentacles, and the slits in its eyes. Then add dimension to the foot tentacles by doubling the lines you used to draw them.

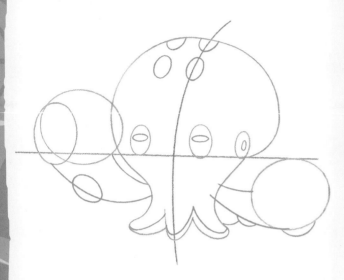

Do you notice any similarities in the steps to draw Clobbopus's two large tentacles and the steps you used to draw Cufant's trunk?

4 Detail dilemma? Don't fret it or sweat it! Use curved lines to draw the mask around Clobbopus's eyes and the pattern on its tentacles.

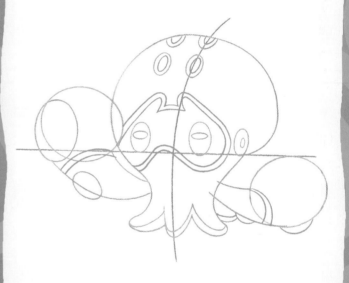

5 Take a look at your final drawing. Do any lines need to be adjusted? Do any marks need to be erased? Do the suction cups on the tentacles look three-dimensional? Does your Pokémon look ready to punch an opponent? Color in your Clobbopus with contrasting hues of purple and orange!

DID YOU KNOW?
If Clobbopus's tentacle gets torn off in battle, it just grows back! If you make a mistake when drawing, you can start over, too.

EEVEE

This Normal-type Pokémon has more possible Evolutions than any other Pokémon! How many can you name? How is your artistic evolution going? This may be a good time to tape up all the drawings you've made so far and check out your progress!

1 There's a lot of joy in Eevee's pose, so keep your guidelines fast, loose, and leaning to the right. Then draw a circle for the head. You're all set up to capture the playful tilt of Eevee's head in the final drawing.

2 Build your Pokémon one basic shape at a time. Attach two shapes for the chest fur to the bottom of the head. Attach the legs below the chest shape. Then draw the ears on top of the head. Now squint your eyes. Does it already look a little like an Eevee? Cool! Go ahead and sketch in the eyes and mouth!

3 Time to level up with details! Add short curved lines to the paws and neck—and more details inside the mouth and eyes. Then add dimension to the ears by doubling their outline. Don't forget to sketch in Evee's big bushy tail.

4 This step is all about using lines to add texture. A few zigzags on the tail, head, and collar will make them look much furrier!

5 Erase any lines you don't need and take a minute to size up your drawing. Do you feel like your skills are evolving?

DRAWING CHALLENGE
Now that you can draw Eevee, try drawing Gigantamax Eevee. How do you show that a Pokémon is big or small in a drawing? It's all about scale. Draw Eevee next to a giant Pokémon like a Snorlax. If Eevee is bigger, it must be Gigantamaxed!

SYLVEON

Sylveon is an evolved form of Eevee, and drawing it can be a challenge. You may want to practice drawing big sweeping S curves before you draw the ribbon-like feelers Sylveon uses to calm down its opponents.

1 Start with guidelines and basic shapes to get an overall sense of Sylveon's body. Then draw a third guideline where you think the ground should be. This line will help you draw the legs in the next step. If you angle the guideline slightly, the back legs will be a tiny bit shorter than the front legs. This is a great trick for making them look farther away.

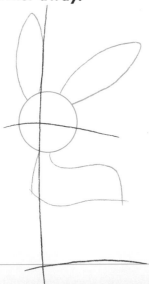

2 Use sweeping lines to sketch in Sylveon's ribbon-like feelers. When you're ready, block in the face and the two legs closest to you. Extend the lines for these legs up and over the shape of the body.

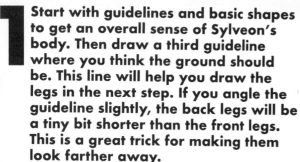

3 Draw the two legs farthest from you. Did you notice that some of the lines are hidden behind the body and other legs? Now add details to the face, paws, and ribbons. Don't forget the bows!

4 Compare your drawing to the one in the book. Do you need to make any changes? Now's the time! Are the legs the right size and shape? Are any details missing? Did you keep the line that separates Sylveon's back right leg from the body? Good job! When you're ready, color this Fairy-type Pokémon in shades of pale pink and blue.

Ready for the next drawing challenge? You'll use lots of S-curves to draw the next few Pokémon!

CENTISKORCH

This Fire- and Bug-type Pokémon is known as the Radiator Pokémon because its body temperature is a scorching 1,500 degrees! It's also known for its fiery temper. But don't get frustrated when making this drawing. Remember those S curves you practiced when learning to draw Sylveon? They'll come in handy here. Centiskorch's body is like one giant letter S!

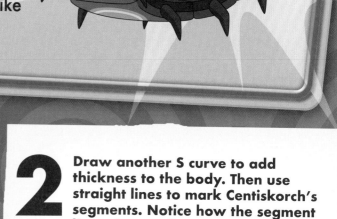

1 Start by sketching an S curve. It's okay if you need to use more than one line to get it down. Then draw an oval for the face. Follow it up with a long curved line that runs from the oval to the tail. Add another line that starts at the tail and ends in the middle of the body. Centiskorch's body is flat, but it still has some thickness. Those blue lines are the key to making it look three-dimensional.

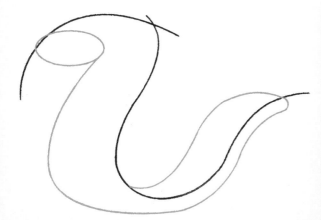

2 Draw another S curve to add thickness to the body. Then use straight lines to mark Centiskorch's segments. Notice how the segment lines change direction on the side of the body? Finish up this step with half-moons for the eyes.

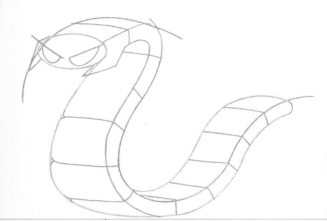

3

Add details to the face and feelers to the body. See how the feelers on the far side are tucked behind the body? Don't forget the upside-down triangle on top of the head.

4

Time to sketch the pattern on the underside of Centiskorch's body—an oval inside an oval fits inside each segment. Then draw the wavy flames of the antennae and tail.

DRAWING TIP

Have you ever stared into a fire? The edges are blurry and wavy. Try using your eraser to smudge the edges of the flames before you add color.

DRAWING CHALLENGE

When Centiskorch Gigantamaxes, the number of segments and legs on its body increases—to a total of 100 legs! That means Gigantamax Centiskorch can move really fast—and causes A LOT of destruction. Try drawing its fiery rampage now!

5

Clean up your drawing and take a good look. Are the antennae and tail fiery? Does Centiskorch look fierce? Get out your red, brown, orange, and yellow colors and get ready to turn up the heat on this drawing!

SILICOBRA

This Sand Snake Pokémon likes to burrow into the ground to hide! But don't hide from this drawing. It uses more of those S curves, circles, and curved lines you've been practicing all along!

1 Start with two guidelines that lean to the left. Then draw an oval inside a circle. The place where the oval and circle overlap will become the vertical guideline for the face. How cool is that?

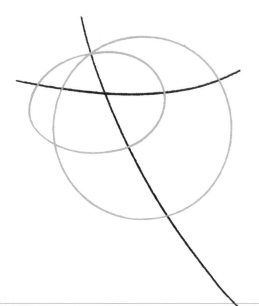

2 Draw another oval at the bottom of the vertical guideline. This will become the curve of the tail. Start reshaping the large circle of the body to create a more cobra-like outline. When you're ready, use the guidelines to help position the eyes.

3 Draw details on the face—like the wavy lines around the eyes that make Silicobra look so sad! Then sketch a wavy line for the mouth and make sure the ends turn down.

LOOK CLOSER
What lines will you use to connect the oval and circle you drew in step two to form a tail?

4 This step is all about adding pattern to the body. Go for it! Don't forget to add the ovals for the nose and the jellybean shapes on its body.

5 Take a beat to clean up your drawing. Does it need any finishing touches? When you're ready, go over the outline with a marker and add color. Then try drawing Silicobra facing off against Sobble. Do you think Silicobra will escape or join the opponent's team?

BONSLY

Looks can be deceiving! Bonsly may seem timid, but they're rock solid underneath it all. They can charm opponents and defend themselves at the same time. The tears they cry aren't about being sad—or tricky. Tears help Bonsly regulate the water in their bodies when the air is really dry. This drawing may look tough, but you can handle it. Rock on!

1 You guessed it—start with guidelines. Then draw a big circle. The bottom of it should touch the horizontal guideline. Draw a smaller circle at the very top of the vertical guideline. Now start on the feet and legs.

Don't forget the guidelines on the face!

2 Start by drawing the circles on top of Bonsly's head. Then move on to the hat and face. Bonsly has a ring around its body just below its mouth.

Ring around the Bonsly! Take a closer look at that waist area.

1	2	3

3 Draw a dark oval inside the eyes. Then draw a short curved line inside the mouth to make it look open. Now add a football-like shape to the top of Bonsly's front leg and a U shape at the top of its back leg. You're almost done!

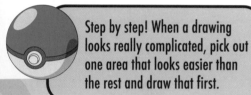
Step by step! When a drawing looks really complicated, pick out one area that looks easier than the rest and draw that first.

4 Erase any lines you don't need— like the bottom of the circle you drew for the head. Phew! Now you can see your drawing and clean up mistakes.

Don't get teary-eyed! Mistakes help you learn and ultimately make you a better artist.

5 Want to make the balls on top of Bonsly's head look 3-D? Add a light yellow-green highlight to the top-left side of each ball and a warmer brown-green crescent-shaped shadow on the bottom right.

NICKIT

This cunning Dark-type Pokémon survives by stealing food from other Pokémon—and Trainers! Then it erases its tracks with a swipe of its tail so no one can follow it! If you have a kneaded eraser, you can mold it into a point to erase those hard-to-reach smudges in the corners of your drawing.

1 The curve of the horizontal guideline is important to this drawing, so take some time to make sure it falls where you need it to. You can even trace the guidelines to get you started. Then add two circles that are about the same size—one for the head and one for the tail!

2 Sketch in the basic shapes of the ears and body. See how the shape of the body cradles the circle you drew for the head? Then draw a triangle for the snout at the base of the head and a half circle for the eye. Take note: most of the face is at the very bottom of the head.

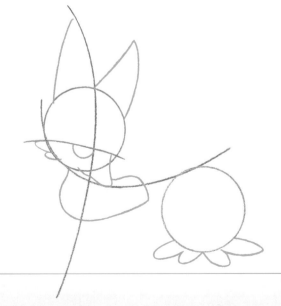

3

Time to make connections. How does the body connect to the bulb of the tail? How do the legs connect to the body?

DRAWING TIP

Study the new blue lines in this step. What suggestions would you give a friend who was trying to draw this Nickit?

LOOK CLOSER

Sometimes making part of a drawing bigger helps you see how the lines fit together. Notice how the corner of the eye falls right where the guidelines crisscross? Don't forget to draw the tongue inside the mouth.

4

Add details on the paws, chest, and face. Nickit has a black patch around its eyes like a mask. Use curved lines to get the shape down.

5

Erase any lines you don't need and take another look at your drawing. Refine your lines and add any finishing touches. See how the black color on Nickit's tail kind of runs into the brown? Try using watercolors to finish off the tail.

SKWOVET

These Cheeky Pokémon are found all over the Galar region. They may look sweet, but they can cause lots of chaos with their unstoppable appetites. Skwovet eat berries NONSTOP! Once, a tiny Skwovet caused a huge squabble on Cerise Island because it kept hoarding all the Pokémon food!

1
Draw a vertical guideline that leans to the left. Then draw a small horizontal guideline closer to the bottom. The starter shapes for Skwovet are two circles, but the biggest one isn't for the head—it's for the tail!

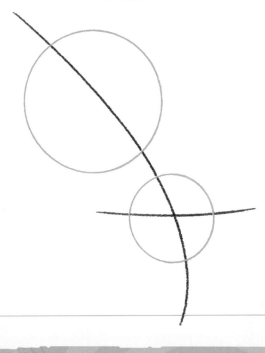

2
Use light, loose lines to sketch in the basic shapes of Skwovet's body. There are lots of half-moons and curves. Then use more half circles for the eyes and nose. See how they rest right on that horizontal guideline?

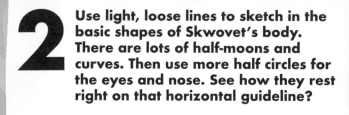

Check out the shape of Skwovet's ears. They kind of look like tulips!

3 Connect the body to the tail with more sweeping curved lines. Then draw the front legs and add details to the face. See how the right leg sits on top of the circle you drew for the body? The left leg is tucked right behind it!

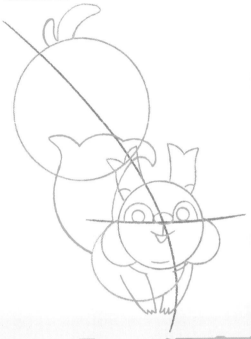

4 Sketch Skwovet's back right leg. Then focus on the details. There are lots of them, so take your time! Can you see the joy in Skwovet's face already?

5 Take a minute to study your drawing. Once you erase the starter shapes, you can see the true outline of Skwovet's big cheeks. Do they look full of berries? Does the tail look big and bushy?

DRAWING CHALLENGE

Where in the Galar region do you imagine you'd find the most Skwovet? Color in a background for your masterpiece!

MIME JR.

Mime Jr., Mimic, now! Mime Jr. likes to mimic the moves of its opponents in battle. Enemies let down their guard because they can't look away. Sometimes, it's just as hard to look away from a drawing you've been struggling with. When this happens, hold your drawing up to a mirror. Looking at it from a different perspective will help you spot mistakes.

1 The guidelines are different in this drawing. The horizontal line curves like the arms of a stick figure. Draw a big oval for the head above the arms and smaller ovals for the hands and body. At this stage, Mime Jr. should look kind of like a snowman.

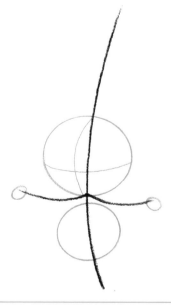

2 Start with ovals for the eyes, nose, and the sides of the hat. Then draw Mime Jr.'s body around the circle you drew in step one. See how helpful basic shapes can be?

There's a lot going on in step two, but don't let it scare you off. Break it down. And take your time!

3

Almost done! Add details like a smiling mouth and dark eyes. Then draw a string of U shapes around Mime Jr.'s waist. Follow the curve of the circle so it looks 3-D.

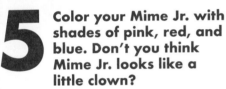

Remember to look back to the Introduction for tips on drawing faces.

4

Great job! Erase any lines you don't need. Now take a minute to look at your drawing. Do you need to make any changes?

Smudge-proof your masterpiece! Keep a piece of scrap paper under your hand as you draw.

5

Color your Mime Jr. with shades of pink, red, and blue. Don't you think Mime Jr. looks like a little clown?

Feeling good? You're ready to move on to the next level. Keep going!

TOXEL

Look, but don't touch! Toxel is an Electric- and Poison-type Pokémon. The poison it secretes through its skin can actually make electricity! But don't let drawing this Baby Pokémon stop you in your tracks! Remember, even the most complicated drawings start out the same way—with simple lines and shapes!

1 Start off by drawing a couple of quick lines to guide your drawing, a straight vertical line and a long curved horizontal line. Then draw a circle for the head and a long U shape for the body. Toxel's eyes sit low on its face, so draw a straight eyeline at the bottom of the circle.

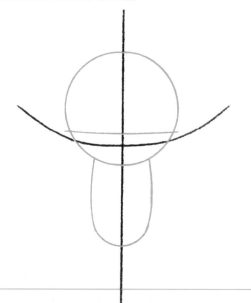

2 Take a beat to get the basic shapes of the body down. Use lots of fluid curved lines for the arms, legs, and neckline. Then draw half circles for the eyes. Toxel has shapes that look like pointy cat ears at the top and sides of its head.

3 Time for details! Where would you like to start? With the lightning bolt on Toxel's head? The curves on the paws? Or the shapes in the body?

4 Add more details to the helmet, eyes, and paws. Take your time. Are you missing anything?

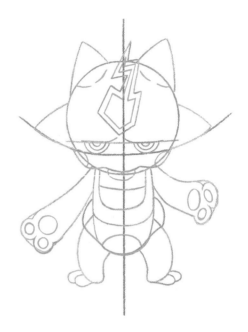

DRAWING TIP

Want to figure out which basic shapes to start with on your own? Squint at the final step of the drawing above. Squinting helps you see the basic shapes because it blocks out all the details.

5 Erase any lines you don't need and take a step back. Feeling electrified? Add any finishing touches, then trace over the outlines with a thin marker or ink pen. Then pick your poison! Will you use markers, crayons, watercolors, or cut paper to color in this purple Pokémon? Get creative!

WEAVILE

Weavile are mischievous Pokémon. They use their sharp claws to carve messages for one another in icy surfaces and on trees. Did you know you could carve out your own drawing style? Every drawing is different, just like every Pokémon's personality is different. What will you do to make this drawing your own? It's a supercharged Pokémon challenge, but you can do it!

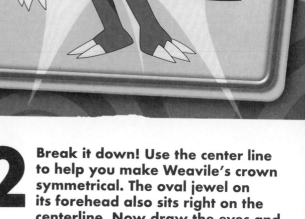

1 Start with a stick figure. Draw the back leg bent and keep the front leg straight so it looks like it's coming forward. The feet and arms are triangles this time instead of ovals.

Weavile's head is tilted down, so the horizontal guideline on the face is all the way at the bottom of the circle you drew for the head. Remember, guidelines on the face curve.

2 Break it down! Use the center line to help you make Weavile's crown symmetrical. The oval jewel on its forehead also sits right on the centerline. Now draw the eyes and ears. They're all shaped like crescent moons!

There are lots of jagged lines in this drawing, like Weavile's sharp claws. Did you practice drawing zigzags in the warm-up?

3 Use this step to fine-tune the outlines of the shapes you drew in steps one and two. This will make Weavile look more realistic. Then draw the tail and add details like the teeth, eyelashes, and lines in the ears.

4 Compare your drawing to the Weavile in the book. Are you missing anything? Make any last-minute adjustments.

LOOK CLOSER

Did you notice that Weavile has three claws on each paw instead of two like Sneasel, its pre-evolved form? Practice drawing Weavile's folded arms on scrap paper.

5 Weavile's dark red eyes match its headgear and tail. But the oval on its forehead is a golden yellow. Color it in first so it doesn't get muddy.

DRAWING CHALLENGE

Draw a pair of Weavile in a snowy forest—where they love to live. What kind of mysterious messages have they carved on the trees?

TYROGUE

Tyrogue are tough for their size. Hotheaded and short-tempered, they slug first and ask questions later. That means that they're often nursing injuries, but their boundless energy keeps them on the attack anyway . . . even against larger foes!

1 In a smooth flowing motion, sketch in the two action lines. The more fluid they appear, the more life your drawing will have. As usual, position the basic shapes . . . head circle, hands, hips.

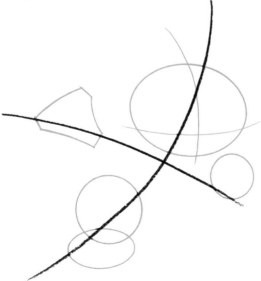

2 This figure may look harder than previous Pokémon, but it's all a matter of doing things in order. First, draw the facial features and add a single blade to the forehead. Next, draw the large kidney bean shape of the raised foot. This will make the rest of the limbs much easier to place and sketch.

3 Fill in the rest of the blades along the top of the head and refine the facial features. Next, focus on sketching in the fingers and clenched fist. Don't forget Tyrogue's left thigh!

4 Finish your drawing in the usual way, but as you darken your linework, try to make your outlines more natural looking . . . more relaxed and not as stiff as the geometric shapes you used to create Tyrogue.

DRAWING TIP
Try drawing your first draft on tracing paper. If you use a layer for each step, you won't have to erase as much.

ALCREMIE

This Fairy-type Pokémon is a dream for Trainers—and an even bigger delight to draw! When Alcremie trusts its Trainer, it treats them to berries. And when Alcremie is happy, the cream it secretes from its hands becomes richer and sweeter. How sweet is it to have mastered so many Pokémon drawings?

1 Remember those circles we drew earlier in the book? Alcremie starts with one, too! Then draw a slanted oval for the body. See how it sits toward the bottom of the vertical guideline?

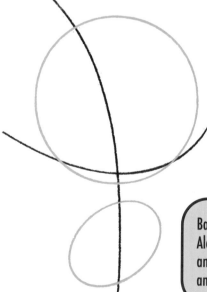

2 There are a lot of details in this drawing, but they can all be broken down into basic lines and shapes—like ovals, wavy lines, and curves. Use the guidelines to help you work out where to draw them.

Basic shapes are like building blocks. Alone, they are circles, ovals, squares, and rectangles, but put them together and they start to build a Pokémon!

3

It's time to sketch in more shapes like the arms, hairline, and gumdrop shapes on the head. See those ovals you drew for the hair in step two? Make their edges wavy to show off Alcremie's creamy decorations.

4

Ready to refine the details? Add tiny ovals to the gumdrops you drew in step three to turn them into berries. Then draw curved lines and crescent shapes all over the body to highlight Alcremie's creamy texture.

5

Now erase the lines you don't need and take a step back. Do you need to do anything to the lines before you start adding color? Use creamy hues for this Fairy type's body and raspberry reds for the eyes, berries, and details.

DRAWING CHALLENGE

Fun fact! Gigantamax Alcremie can launch missiles made of highly caloric cream! If you could draw Gigatamax Alcremie battling any Pokémon in the Galar region, which one would it be?

CONGRATULATIONS!

You've practiced drawing 43 different Pokémon! How do you feel?

What do you want to draw next?

Here are a few ideas:

- Try setting up a gallery of all your drawings from oldest to newest. Can you see the progress you've made? List three things you've learned about drawing Pokémon from this book.

- Make your own artistic Pokédex! Set up a sketchbook just for your Pokémon art and draw a different Pokémon on each page.

- Try drawing a group scene of your top three favorite Pokémon. Or a battle between your two dream Pokémon. Or even your Pokémon BFFs hanging out on Cerise Island with Pikachu. The possibilities are endless!

What are your ideas? What do you want your next challenge to be?

Keep practicing! Keep learning! And keep drawing!